For Tom Morrison (1944–1994)

Fireflies are not flies, but soft-bodied beetles.
They have a luminous, light-giving organ that
blinks on and off in the night to attract other
fireflies. This light is a "cold" light;
it does not give off any heat—
something that has scientists puzzled.

There are about 2,000 species of fireflies
in the world, of which approximately 50 can
be found in the United States.

Dear Parents and Educators,

Welcome to Penguin Young Readers! As parents and educators, you know that each child develops at his or her own pace—in terms of speech, critical thinking, and, of course, reading. Penguin Young Readers recognizes this fact. As a result, each Penguin Young Readers book is assigned a traditional easy-to-read level (1–4) as well as a Guided Reading Level (A–P). Both of these systems will help you choose the right book for your child. Please refer to the back of each book for specific leveling information. Penguin Young Readers features esteemed authors and illustrators, stories about favorite characters, fascinating nonfiction, and more!

The Very Lonely Firefly

LEVEL **2**

GUIDED
READING
LEVEL **I**

This book is perfect for a **Progressing Reader** who:
- can figure out unknown words by using picture and context clues;
- can recognize beginning, middle, and ending sounds;
- can make and confirm predictions about what will happen in the text; and
- can distinguish between fiction and nonfiction.

Here are some **activities** you can do during and after reading this book:
- Compound Words: A compound word is made when two words are joined together to form a new word. *Firefly* is a compound word used in this story. Reread the story and try to find other compound words.
- Adding -ing to Words: With many -ing words, the ending is simply added to the root word, as in flicker/flickering. But when a word ends with an *e*, it is removed before adding the -ing ending, as in shine/shining. Reread the story and try to find all the words that end with -ing. On a separate sheet of paper, write the root word for each word. For example, reflecting/reflect.

Remember, sharing the love of reading with a child is the best gift you can give!

—Bonnie Bader, EdM
Penguin Young Readers program

*Penguin Young Readers are leveled by independent reviewers applying the standards developed by Irene Fountas and Gay Su Pinnell in *Matching Books to Readers: Using Leveled Books in Guided Reading*, Heinemann, 1999.

Penguin Young Readers
Published by the Penguin Group
Penguin Group (USA) Inc., 375 Hudson Street, New York, New York 10014, USA
Penguin Group (Canada), 90 Eglinton Avenue East, Suite 700, Toronto, Ontario M4P 2Y3, Canada
(a division of Pearson Penguin Canada Inc.)
Penguin Books Ltd., 80 Strand, London WC2R 0RL, England
Penguin Group Ireland, 25 St. Stephen's Green, Dublin 2, Ireland (a division of Penguin Books Ltd.)
Penguin Group (Australia), 250 Camberwell Road, Camberwell, Victoria 3124, Australia
(a division of Pearson Australia Group Pty. Ltd.)
Penguin Books India Pvt. Ltd., 11 Community Centre, Panchsheel Park, New Delhi—110 017, India
Penguin Group (NZ), 67 Apollo Drive, Rosedale, Auckland 0632, New Zealand
(a division of Pearson New Zealand Ltd.)
Penguin Books (South Africa) (Pty.) Ltd., 24 Sturdee Avenue,
Rosebank, Johannesburg 2196, South Africa

Penguin Books Ltd., Registered Offices: 80 Strand, London WC2R 0RL, England

The Library of Congress has cataloged the Philomel edition
under the following Control Number: 94027827

ISBN 978-0-448-45850-2 (pbk)   10 9 8 7 6 5 4 3 2 1
ISBN 978-0-448-45851-9 (hc)   10 9 8 7 6 5 4 3 2 1

ALWAYS LEARNING   PEARSON

PENGUIN YOUNG READERS

LEVEL

2

PROGRESSING READER

The Very Lonely Firefly

by Eric Carle

Penguin Young Readers
An Imprint of Penguin Group (USA) Inc.

As the sun set

a little firefly was born.

It stretched its wings

and flew off into

the darkening sky.

It was a lonely firefly,

and it flashed its light

searching for other fireflies.

The firefly saw a light
and flew toward it.

But it was not another firefly.

It was a lightbulb

lighting up the night.

The firefly saw a light
and flew toward it.

But it was not another firefly.

It was a candle

flickering in the night.

The firefly saw a light

and flew toward it.

But it was not another firefly.

It was a flashlight

shining in the night.

The firefly saw a light

and flew toward it.

But it was not another firefly.

It was a lantern

glowing in the night.

The firefly saw several lights
and flew toward them.

But they were not other fireflies.

There was a dog and...

a cat and...

an owl,

their eyes reflecting

the lights.

The firefly saw a light

and flew toward it.

But it was not another firefly.

It was a car's headlights

flooding the night.

The firefly saw many lights

and flew toward them.

But they were not other fireflies.

They were fireworks

sparkling and glittering

and shimmering in the night.

When all was quiet,

the firefly flew through the night

flashing its light,

looking and searching again.

Then the very lonely firefly saw

what it had been looking for...

a group of fireflies,

flashing *their* lights.

Now the firefly wasn't

lonely anymore.